Dear Parent:

Psst . . . you're looking at the *Super Secret Weapon of Reading*. It's called comics.

STEP INTO READING® COMIC READERS are a perfect step in learning to read. They provide visual cues to the meaning of words and helpfully break out short pieces of dialogue into speech balloons.

Here are some terms commonly associated with comics:

PANEL: A section of a comic with a box drawn around it.
CAPTION: Narration that helps set the scene.
SPEECH BALLOON: A bubble containing dialogue.
GUTTER: The space between panels.

Tips for reading comics with your child:

• Have your child read the speech balloons while you read the captions.
• Ask your child: What is a character feeling? How can you tell?
• Have your child draw a comic showing what happens after the book is finished.

STEP INTO READING® COMIC READERS are designed to engage and to provide an empowering reading experience. They are also fun. The best-kept secret of comics is that they create lifelong readers. *And that will make you the real hero of the story!*

Jennifer L. Holm and Matthew Holm
Co-creators of the Babymouse and Squish series

The Dream-tastic Story Collection

Special thanks to Venetia Davie, Ryan Ferguson, Charnita Belcher, Julia Phelps, Nicole Corse, Sharon Woloszyk, Rob, Hudnut, Shelley Dvi-Vardhana, Michelle Cogan and Gabrielle Miles

Published in the United States by Random House Children's Books, a division of Random House LLC, 1745 Broadway, New York, NY 10019, and in Canada by Random House of Canada Limited, Toronto, Penguin Random House Companies.

The works in this collection were originally published seperately in the United States by Random House Children's Books in slightly different form as *Dream Closet*, copyright © 2013 Mattel; *Happy Birthday, Chelsea!*, copyright © 2013 Mattel; *Too Many Puppies!*, copyright © 2014 Mattel; and *Licensed to Drive*, copyright © 2014 Mattel.

Visit us on the Web!
StepIntoReading.com
randomhousekids.com

Educators and librarians, for a variety of teaching tools, visit us at RHTeachersLibrarians.com
ISBN 978-0-553-52337-9
MANUFACTURED IN CHINA
10 9 8 7 6 5 4 3 2 1

Barbie
Life in the Dreamhouse

The Dream-tastic Story Collection

Step 3 Books

A Collection of Four Comic Readers

Random House 🏠 New York

Barbie

Life in the Dreamhouse

Hi, I'm Barbie! I hope you enjoy these four dream-tastic stories!

Contents

Barbie
Life in the
Dreamhouse

Dream Closet

A COMIC READER

Adapted by Kristen L. Depken

Based on the screenplay by Robin Stein

Random House New York

At the Dreamhouse, Nikki and Teresa are helping Barbie pick out an outfit.

I want to look perfect for my date with Ken.

It's our forty-third anniversary—of the first time we held hands!

Barbie can't wait for her date!
Her outfit is almost perfect.

My little rhinestone-studded butterfly barrette.

Barbie's closet . . .

is . . .

AMAZING!

Meanwhile . . .

Barbie gives Teresa and Nikki a tour of her closet.

I've got clothes from every career I've ever had.

24

Actually, Teresa, it's a great way for me to test new hair and makeup looks.

Ooh! Sounds like fun.

Let's try it!

They get right to work. . . .

Hours later . . .

Back in the closet . . .

Mondo Barbie Head is looking good!

Can't say the same about us!

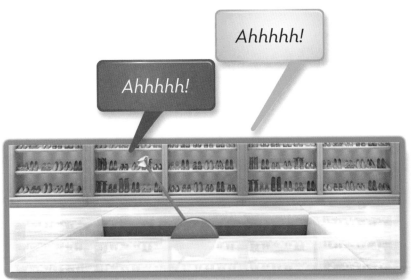

They slide
down a long dark chute . . .

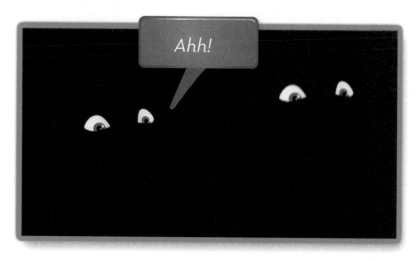

and land on Barbie's front steps!

Thanks for all your help, girls! You're the best friends ever!

Barbie
Life in the
Dreamhouse

Happy Birthday, Chelsea!

A COMIC READER

Adapted by Mary Tillworth

Based on the screenplay by David Wiebe

Random House 🏠 New York

It's a special morning.
Barbie, Skipper, and Stacie
are getting ready for
Chelsea's birthday!

Chelsea

It's my birthday.
It's finally here!

Places, everyone.

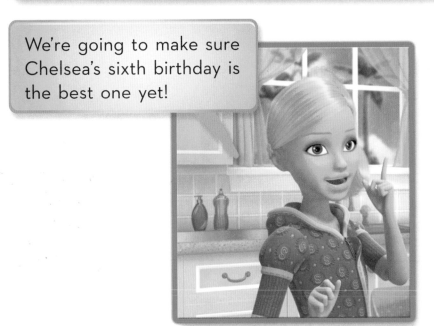

We're going to make sure Chelsea's sixth birthday is the best one yet!

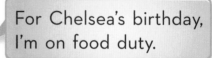
For Chelsea's birthday, I'm on food duty.

Barbie, you're in charge of distracting Chelsea.

Skipper, you're on decorating duty.

Awww. Can't Ken do it?

Ken's in the garage putting Chelsea's gift together.

It's a bike!

All Chelsea ever talks about is getting a bike.

She is going to be so surprised!

Hmm . . .

The birthday girl appears!

A special birthday breakfast . . .
for a special birthday girl!

This is all great.
But what I really want
for my birthday is to . . .

Grrble. Frrble.

You're welcome.

Back in the kitchen,
Stacie makes the cake.

Ding!

Baking can be hard work.

And in the living room,
Skipper does the decorating.

Why do I always have the hardest job?

Click!

There are balloons . . .

streamers . . .

and a piñata!

Back in the garage,
Ken has his own problems. . . .

Barbie, you write down each gift and who it's from.

Skipper, you're on recycling duty.

Aw, come on!

75

This has been the bestest day!

The yummy cake . . .

the decorations . . .

the presents . . .

But . . .

But?

I just wanted . . .

A unicorn?

All I really wanted was a tennis-playing robot.

Thud!

Too Many Puppies!

A COMIC READER

Adapted by Mary Tillworth

Based on the screenplay by David Wiebe

Random House 🏠 New York

It is another beautiful morning
at the Dreamhouse.

Hmm . . . Nikki's blog said these earrings were the next big thing, huh? I don't know. . . .

I think they look amazing!

Barbie! Barbie! You've got to come down! Taffy's puppies are coming!

Gasp! We need a vet!

gymnast . . .

news reporter . . .

Barbie, hurry!

. . . chef, scuba diver, ballerina . . .

Vet! Vet!

Delivery for 1959 Malibu Way!

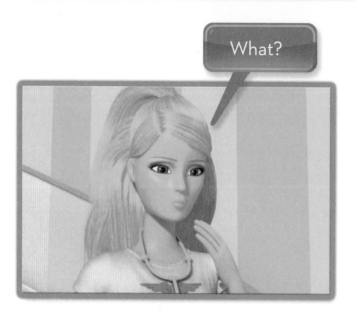

Ruff! Ruff!

Oh, it's darling!

Whenever I get close to anything adorable, well . . .

I . . . faint.

It's quite common.

Teach them tricks!

Walk them.

Teach them to swim. . . .

Potty-train them!

Better move that to the top of the list.

The puppies are adorable . . .

but not . . . as
adorable as me!

Pop!

This cat doesn't play around!

Guys, I love these pooches as much as you do . . .

but we can't keep all these puppies!

How about putting them up for adoption?

Oh, they're
so cute!

Ruff! Ruff! Ruff!

Uh . . .

Thud!

Hey, Barbie! I had this great idea for this awesome song. . . .

Aagh!

Hey, they look good on you, Ryan. Care to adopt one?

They look good on me? I'll take them all!

If you say so!

Ruff! Ruff!

Ruff!

Ruff! Ruff!

Later . . .

This couldn't get any less cool.

Licensed to Drive

Adapted by Mary Tillworth

Based on the screenplay by David Wiebe

Random House 🏠 New York

It is a quiet afternoon
in Barbie's Dreamhouse.

Gasp!

Eeeeee!!!

I heard the squeal!

My driver's license!

You know, I've had so many careers . . .

It's hard to keep track of all one hundred and thirty-five of them!

And counting!

Ring!
Ring!

Hello?

We heard the squeal.
Did you get it?

The forecast calls for sunny . . .

with a chance of a whole lot of cute guys!

I have my license, but the truth is . . .

I never learned how to drive.

I heard the squeal!

I'll call you later.

Sooo . . . where is it?

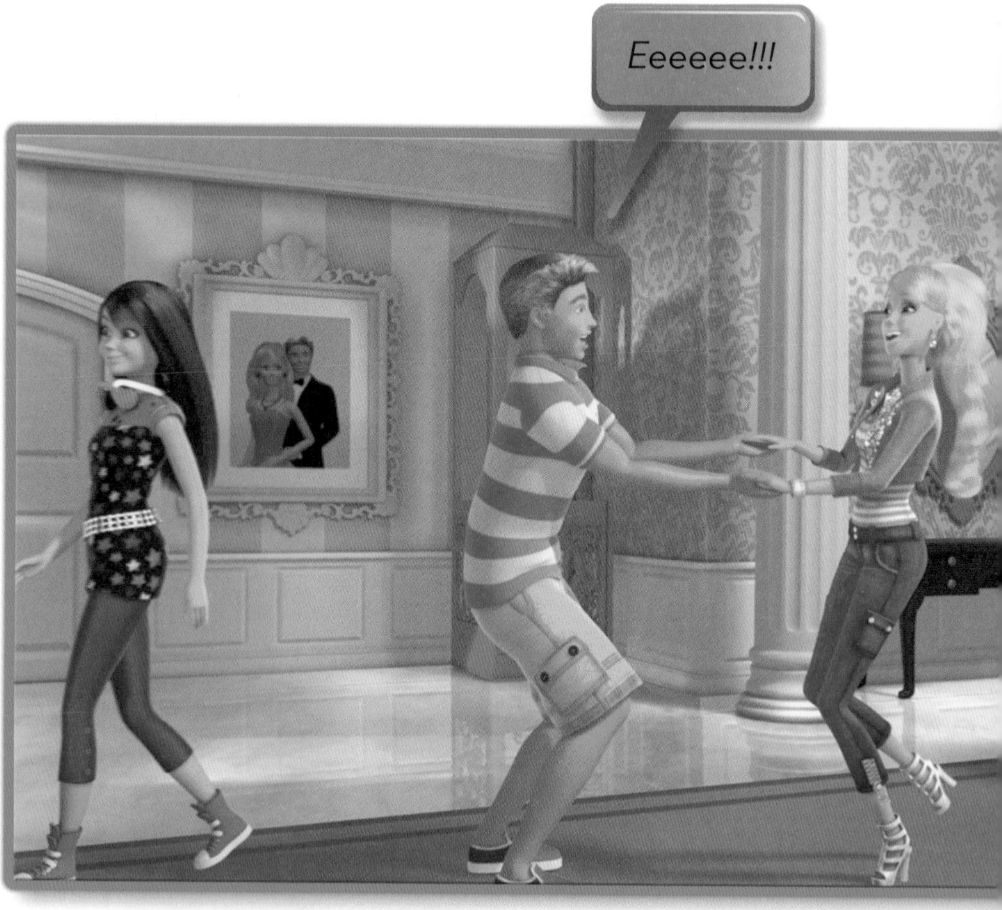
Eeeeee!!!

You've been waiting a long time for this.

So I wanted to give you something for this special occasion.

Gasp!

It's gorgeous!

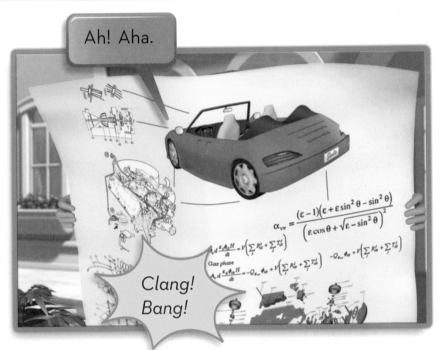

Now for a quick check of the mirrors . . .

And we're ready to go.

Screech!!!

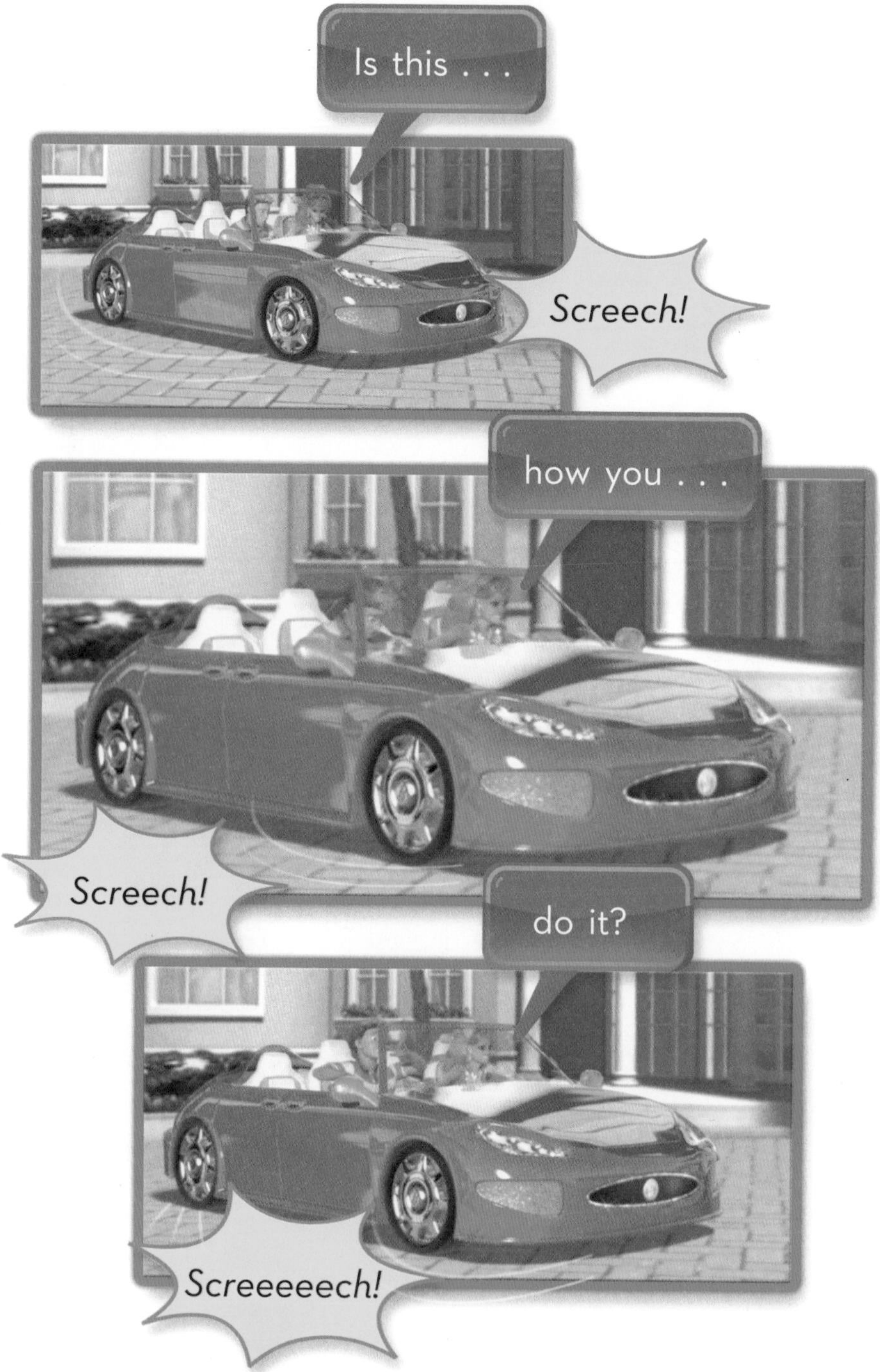
Is this . . .
Screech!
how you . . .
Screech!
do it?
Screeeeech!

Later on . . .

I don't know what I was so worried about.

Ja-jing! Ja-jing!

Ja-jing!

Hi, Barbie!

Clunk!

I'll never learn to drive.

It's that darn *schland poofah*!

To the beach!

Well, I'm still not very good at this whole driving thing. . . .

Barbie! Wait!!!

Clunk, clunk, clunk!

What in the world?

Waaaiiit . . .

Warning. Objects in the mirror . . .

may be handsomer than they appear.

Vroom!

Screech!